LITTLE MISS
BRAVE

Roger Hargreaves

Original concept by
Roger Hargreaves

Written and illustrated by
Adam Hargreaves

Little Miss Brave lived in a house built on the edge of a cliff.

She was not afraid of heights!

Unlike Mr Strong.

She was also not afraid of thunderstorms.

Unlike Little Miss Bossy.

Nor was she scared of spiders.

Unlike Mr Tall.

She was not scared of lions or tigers or snakes.

She was not scared of lions and tigers and snakes all in one room.

She was not even scared of lions and tigers and snakes all in one room … in the dark!

Little Miss Brave did not hesitate if someone needed help.

Like saving Mr Wrong from his capsizing bath.

And Little Miss Brave was so brave she even made Mr Brave feel a bit inadequate!

But this was not all.

She was not afraid of speaking her mind when she saw someone doing something they shouldn't.

She was also not afraid of Mr Rude's unkindness.

Like the time he was rude to Little Miss Shy.

Or of pranksters like Little Miss Trouble

And she was not afraid of standing up for others.

Like the time Little Miss Bossy shouted at Little Miss Shy for speaking too quietly.

Little Miss Shy so wished she could be more like Little Miss Brave.

To say thank you, she took Little Miss Brave out
for a picnic.

As they sat munching on their sandwiches a shadow
suddenly fell across them.

"Oh no," said Little Miss Brave. "It's clouding over."

But it wasn't a cloud.

It was a whopping great ...

… giant!

A real-life giant.

A real-life giant in a really bad mood.

"You took my golden eggs!" roared the giant, pointing an enormous finger at Little Miss Brave.

"I … I … don't think so," stammered Little Miss Brave.

"Well, that's not what Little Miss Trouble told me! She told me that you stole my eggs!"

"Hang on just a minute!" interrupted Little Miss Shy, stepping between Little Miss Brave and the giant. "Little Miss Brave has been with me all day and I know that she did not take any golden eggs. And if you believe anything Little Miss Trouble tells you then you're just … silly!"

"Oh," said the giant, who was lost for words.

"And now I think you should apologise and then we'll say no more about this," finished Little Miss Shy.

And the giant did apologise and he and Little Miss Brave shook hands to show there were no hard feelings.

"Well, I never," said Little Miss Brave, in admiration after the Giant left.

"I … I don't know what came over me," blushed Little Miss Shy.

"You were very brave," said Little Miss Brave.

"Very brave, or …"

"... very foolish!" giggled Little Miss Shy.